Cardiff Libraries
www.cardiff.gov.uk/libraries

Llyfrgelloedd Caerdydd
www.caerdydd.gov.uk/llyfrgelloedd

Willow
Tree

A CIP catalogue record for this book is
available from the British Library

This edition published by Willow Tree Books, 2019
Willow Tree Books, Tide Mill Way, Woodbridge, Suffolk, IP12 1AP

0 2 4 6 8 9 7 5 3 1

Text © 2019 Elizabeth Dale
Illustration © Willow Tree Books

Willow Tree Books and associated logos are trademarks and/or
registered trademarks of Imagine That Group Ltd

Written by Elizabeth Dale
Illustrated by Patrick Corrigan

ISBN: 978-1-78958-039-6
Printed in China

www.willowtreebooks.net

For my wonderful grandson, Leo, with much love
E.D.

SAVE the DAY for Ada May!

Notes for grown-ups

To enjoy this book together, first get comfy with your child.
Let them hold the book if they can. Help them if necessary.

Explain that they can be a hero and save the day for
Ada May by doing special actions.

Read the story and look at the pictures together. Encourage your
child to do each action, with help from you if they need it.
Then turn the page to discover what happens next. They will
soon be saving the day for Ada May all on their own!

Written by
**Elizabeth
Dale**

Illustrated by
**Patrick
Corrigan**

Max loves taking his little sister,
Ada May, out in her buggy.

Most of all they like feeding the ducks.

UH-OH!
Max has knocked the buggy!

QUICK!
Save the day for Ada May!
Tip the book towards you before
she falls in the river.

YOU DID IT!

You stopped Ada May from falling
in the river.

UH-OH!

You tipped the book too much!
She's going to crash
into that dog.

Save the day for Ada May!
Turn the book like a wheel.
Steer the buggy around the dog.

YOU DID IT!

You stopped Ada May from crashing into the dog.

UH-OH!

Now she's heading towards the busy road!

HURRY!

Save the day for Ada May!

Tip the book to roll the rock in front of the buggy.

YOU DID IT!

The buggy hit the rock and stopped.

But it stopped so suddenly that Ada May has flown up into the air ...

... and into a tree!
UH-OH!
She's stuck up there!

Save the day for Ada May! Put your mouth near the page and blow her down!

How will she get out
of the trailer?

Save the day
for Ada May!

Slap the book to warn the farmer.
Make him stop!

YOU DID IT!

You made the farmer stop the tractor. But he stopped it so fast that the trailer door flew open.

UH-OH!

The sheep are escaping and so is Ada May!

The farmer needs help to round up the sheep!

Call his dog. 'Help, dog! Help!'

Go on!

LOUDER!

YOU DID IT!

The dog helped to round up the sheep. Clever dog!

UH-OH!

Ada May has crawled into a field.

There's something BIG
in there with her!

Can you guess what it is?

You have to scare it away!

Save the day for Ada May!

Make funny faces!
STAMP YOUR FEET!

LOOK!

There's a gate!

UH-OH! Ada May is too small to climb over it.

Save the day for Ada May!

Lift the book up to help her over the gate!

YOU DID IT!
you lifted Ada May out of the bull's field.

UH-OH!

She's landed on top of a hedge.
She can't climb down.
Save the day for Ada May!

Shake the
book!

Shake it
again!

UH-OH!

She's landed on a roof. How will she get down?
Save the day for Ada May!

Turn the book upside down
and tap the cover hard!

YOU DID IT!

You got Ada May off the roof.

But where's she going to land?

Turn the page to find out!

YOU DID IT!

Look! Ada May has landed back in her buggy.

You saved the day for Ada May!
You're awesome! Give yourself a clap!

'Poor you!' says Max to his little sister. 'You missed all the fun, stuck in your buggy.'

Ada May just smiled. She'd had the most fun of all!